The Berenstain Bears
GO ON VACATION

Welcome to
Gull Island

The Berenstain Bears
Go on Vacation

Stan & Jan Berenstain
with Mike Berenstain

HARPER

An Imprint of HarperCollinsPublishers

When summer begins
and school is done,
the Bears go down
to the sea for fun.

They pack the car
with seashore things:
for baby Honey,
water wings,
flippers for Sister,
a surfboard for Brother,
a comfy inner tube
for Mother,
tackle for Papa,
who loves to fish.
To catch a big one
is his fondest wish.

They drive and drive
and drive and drive.
They wonder if
they'll ever arrive.
Brother asks Papa,
"Will we be there soon?
It's getting late
in the afternoon."

SHORE POINTS

"Mmm . . . mmm!"
says Papa Bear.
"Take a deep breath!
Smell that salt air!

"Just over this bridge,
and across the bay
is the special place
where we will stay!"

They see the sea.
They hear its roar.
There is something special
about the shore.
It soothes the spirit.
It clears the mind.
You can leave your cares
and worries behind.

Up ahead is the house
where the Bears will stay—
on one side, the ocean,
on the other, the bay.

They go inside.
They look around.
All they can hear
is the ocean's sound.
The house is warm
from the afternoon sun.
The Bears' vacation
has now begun.

There is still time
for an afternoon dip.
Into their swimsuits
they hurriedly slip.

"This way!" cries Papa.
"And shake a leg!
The last one in
is a rotten egg!"

A great wave knocks them
head over heels.
How wonderfully cold
and tingly it feels.

Baby Honey and Mama
watch the fun,
sitting in a pool
warmed by the sun.

Then, after eating a quick supper
and climbing into their beds,
they're asleep when the pillows
touch their heads.

When they wake in the morning,
what greets their eyes?
That glorious sight:
a seashore sunrise.
The sun rising from
its ocean bed
paints the sky
a rosy red.

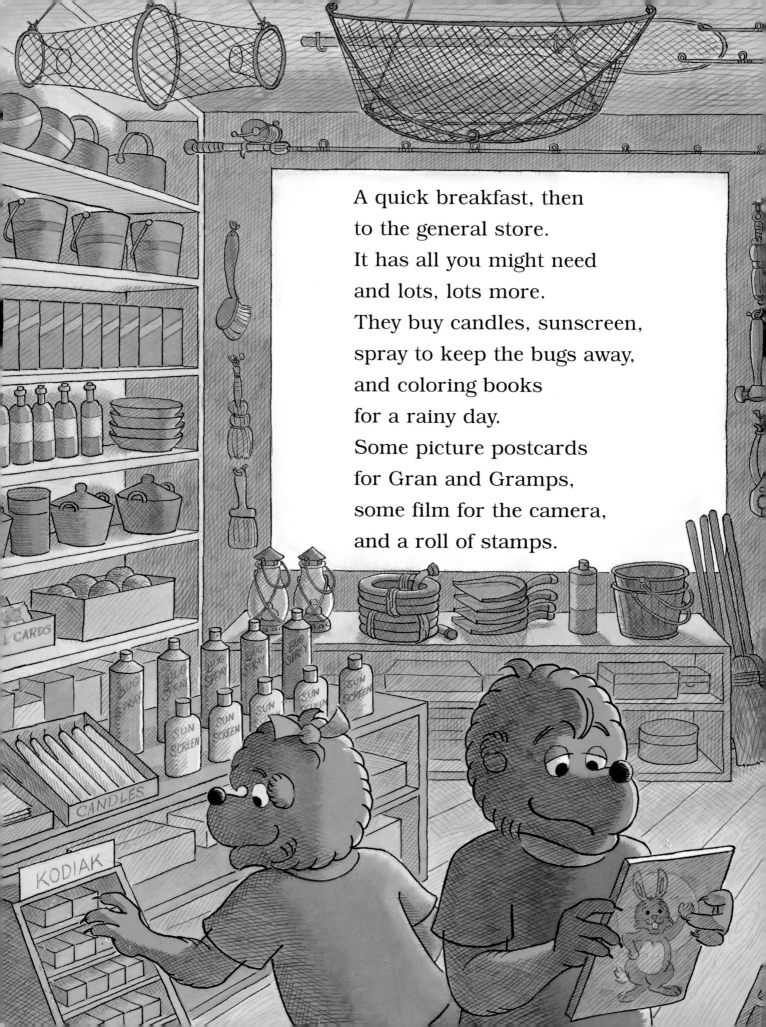

A quick breakfast, then
to the general store.
It has all you might need
and lots, lots more.
They buy candles, sunscreen,
spray to keep the bugs away,
and coloring books
for a rainy day.
Some picture postcards
for Gran and Gramps,
some film for the camera,
and a roll of stamps.

Then back to the house
without delay,
and down to the beach
for a big beach day.

The Bears ride the waves,
they swim, they float,
they wave to bears
in a fishing boat.

They cover Papa with sand
until all that shows
are his eyes, his ears,
his mouth, and his nose.

With buckets of sea
they wet down the sand
and build a castle
so mighty and grand
that it will be ready
for whatever befalls,
or anyone trying
to breach its walls.

Then, hungry as bears
at the end of the day,
they go to dinner
at Gull Island Café,
where plates are heaped high
with the fruit-of-the-sea.
Pa tries the hot sauce—
"WATER! WATER!"
is his pitiful plea.

And at the end of
a hard day's fun,
the Bears' first seashore day
now is done.

In the morning the shore
is shrouded in fog.
The beach is closed,
so they go for a jog.

It looks like rain.
The sky is gray.
What can the Bears do
on a cold, rainy day?

There's more to the shore
than the sand and the sea.
Gull Island Museum
is the place they should be.

There's so much to see:
a whaler's harpoon,
the jaw of a shark,
a Spanish doubloon,
a pirate flag,
tattered and torn,
a thing once thought to be
a unicorn's horn
that's really the tusk
of a kind of whale,
the model of a ship
that was lost in a gale,
the splintered oar
of a whaler's dory.
Each thing they see
tells them a story.

S. S. BEARQUOD
Lost at Sea—1854

"Come, cubs!" says Papa
on another day.
"Let's all go fishing
in Gull Island Bay."

Says Mama Bear,
"Honey and I will stay behind,
so go and have fun.
We don't mind."

The Bears rent a boat.
They climb aboard.
Pa starts the engine
by pulling the cord.

He helps Brother and Sister
with the bait.
They drop their hooks
and patiently wait.

They wait so long
that Pa falls asleep.
The Bears catch some fish,
but they're too small to keep.

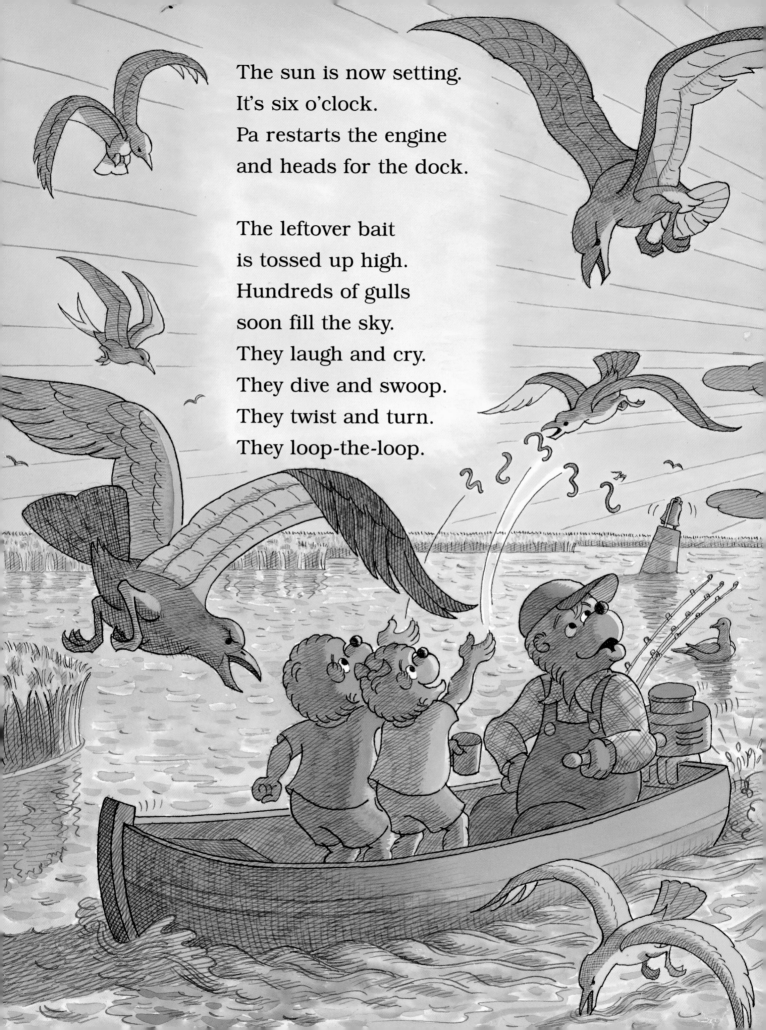

The sun is now setting.
It's six o'clock.
Pa restarts the engine
and heads for the dock.

The leftover bait
is tossed up high.
Hundreds of gulls
soon fill the sky.
They laugh and cry.
They dive and swoop.
They twist and turn.
They loop-the-loop.

Their feeding frenzy
soon is done,
and off they fly
toward the setting sun.

It's fisher-bear Mama
who turns out the winner.
She fished from the beach
and caught a whopper for dinner.

The sun and the sea,
the seashore weather,
all somehow seem
to run together—
the night so cool,
the noonday heat
making the sand
too hot for bear feet.
The ocean's roar
that lulls them to sleep
as they dream about
the mysterious deep
where giant squid,
never seen alive,
swim the great ocean depths
too deep to dive.

And so as the sun
sets over the bay,
the Bears come to the end
of their seashore stay.
Oh, what a wonderful
time they've had!
As they say good-bye,
they feel a bit sad.
But the Bears know
as they go on their way
that the sand and the sea
are here to stay
and they will return
another fine day.